With thanks to William Henry Davies.

What is this life if, full of care,
We have no time to stand and stare.
No time to stand beneath the boughs
And stare as long as sheep or cows.
No time to see, when woods we pass,
Where squirrels hide their nuts in grass.
No time to see, in broad daylight,
Streams full of stars, like skies at night.
No time to turn at Beauty's glance,
And watch her feet, how they can dance.
No time to wait till her mouth can
Enrich that smile her eyes began.
A poor life this if, full of care,
We have no time to stand and stare.

— *Leisure* by W. H. Davies

American edition published in 2018 by Andersen Press USA,
an imprint of Andersen Press Ltd.
www.andersenpressusa.com

First published in Great Britain
in 2018 by Andersen Press Ltd.,
20 Vauxhall Bridge Road, London SW1V 2SA.

Distributed in the United States and Canada by
Lerner Publishing Group, Inc.
241 First Avenue North
Minneapolis, MN 55401 USA
For reading levels and more information, look up this title at www.lernerbooks.com.

Color separated in Switzerland by Photolitho AG, Zürich.
Printed and bound in Malaysia.

Library of Congress Cataloging-in-Publication Data Available
ISBN: 978-1-5415-3554-1
eBook ISBN: 978-1-5415-3555-8

1 –TWP–6/5/18

ELMER'S WALK

David McKee

Andersen Press USA

Elmer the patchwork elephant was sniffing some flowers when some other elephants hurried by. "Come and smell these flowers," Elmer called. "We don't have time, Elmer," said an elephant. "We're hurrying somewhere."

Not long after that, Elmer was looking
at an old tree trunk.
Three crocodiles charged past.
"Hey, crocodiles," called Elmer. "Look, there's
a log pretending to be one of you."
"Another time, Elmer," shouted a crocodile. And
one after another, they plunged into the water
and disappeared.

Lion came running past while Elmer was
listening to the waterfall.
"Hey ho, Lion," said Elmer. "Come and—"
"I don't have time now, Elmer," Lion interrupted.
"I'm late for a very important nap."
Then he was gone.

The monkeys came swinging
through the trees just as Elmer noticed a
spider's web that had captured some drops of rain.
"Look," called Elmer.
"Yes, yes! Lovely! Delightful! Amazing!" said the
monkeys without looking or slowing down.

Continuing his walk, Elmer paused to watch the river play
with his reflection. The group of elephants raced by again.
"Stop a moment," said Elmer.
Before he could say more, an elephant said, "No time,
Elmer. Sorry, we're still hurrying somewhere."
Elmer was alone again.

When the birds flew by, Elmer had no chance to say anything about the rocks he was looking at.

They flew past quickly
with just a, "Hello, Elmer. No time to stop!"
Elmer sighed and walked on.

Suddenly, a noise made Elmer think the
elephants were back. It was the hippos.
"Look at the clouds," said Elmer. "There's
one that looks like an elephant."
"That's funny, Elmer, so do you," said a hippo.
The others laughed and ran on without even
a glance at the clouds.

Elmer was watching the
butterflies dance when Tiger galloped by.
"Steady, Tiger," said Elmer.
Tiger slowed and said, "Elephants may not
know about teatime, but tigers certainly do.
And I don't intend to miss it. No time to stop.
Sorry, bye."

Later, Elmer met Snake.
"You know, Snake," he said, "it's sad.
Nobody has time to just stop and stare."
"I agree," said Snake. "Sad, very sad."
"For instance," said Elmer. "Look at those flowers.
They have more colors than you and I put
together." But snake had already left.

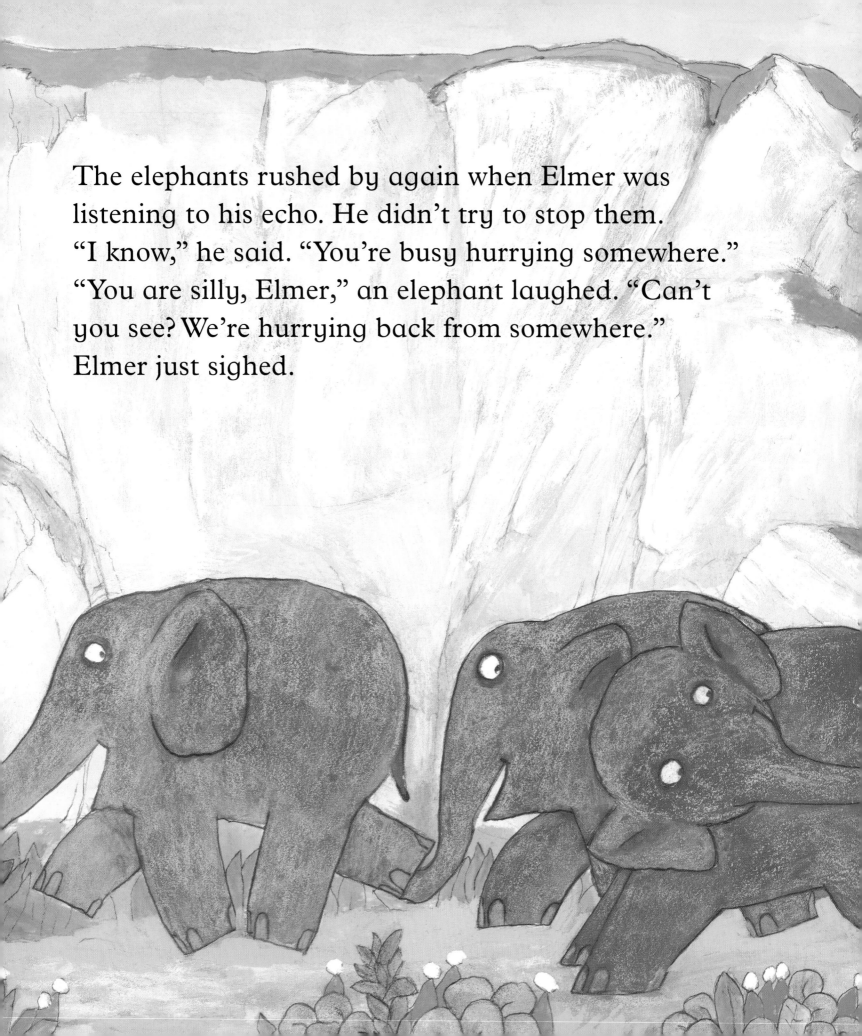

The elephants rushed by again when Elmer was listening to his echo. He didn't try to stop them. "I know," he said. "You're busy hurrying somewhere." "You are silly, Elmer," an elephant laughed. "Can't you see? We're hurrying back from somewhere." Elmer just sighed.

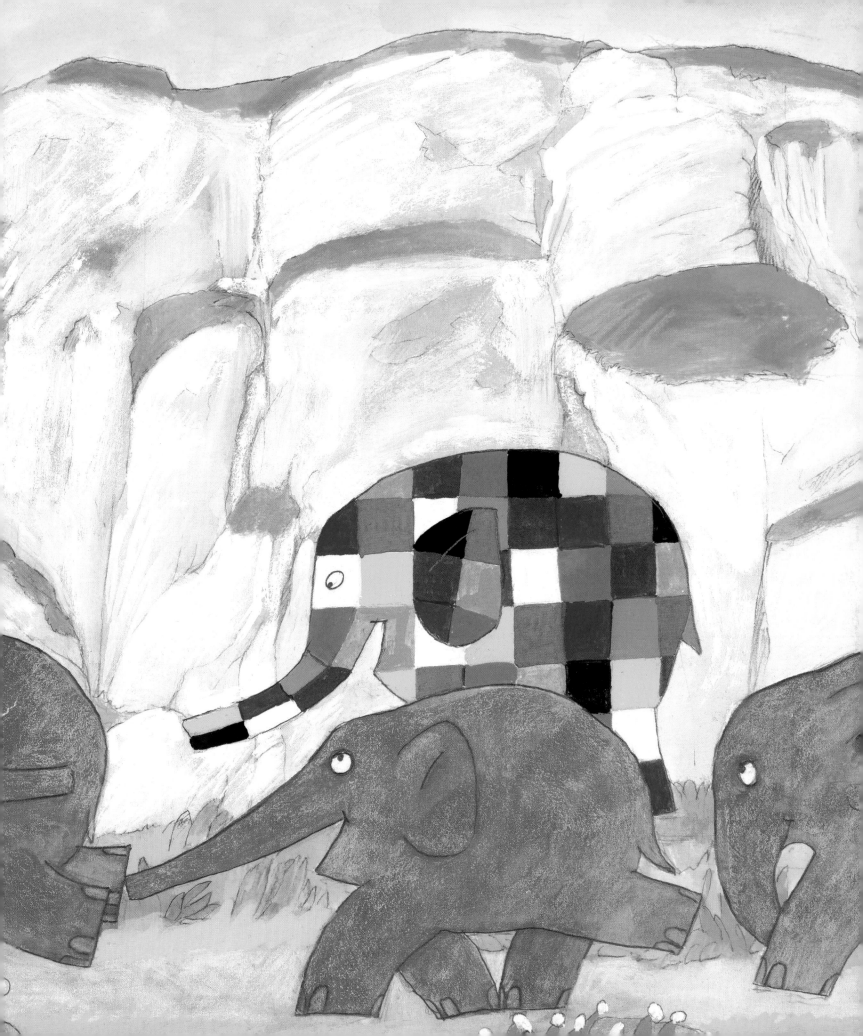

"Hurry, hurry. Hurry, hurry," murmured Elmer
as he strolled on. Then he saw his cousin Wilbur.

"Hello, Wilbur," he said. "What are you doing?"
"Watching the night arrive," said Wilbur.

The cousins stood happily together and
watched the sky darken and fill with stars.

"Shall we count them?" asked Wilbur.

"No," said Elmer. "We haven't the time."